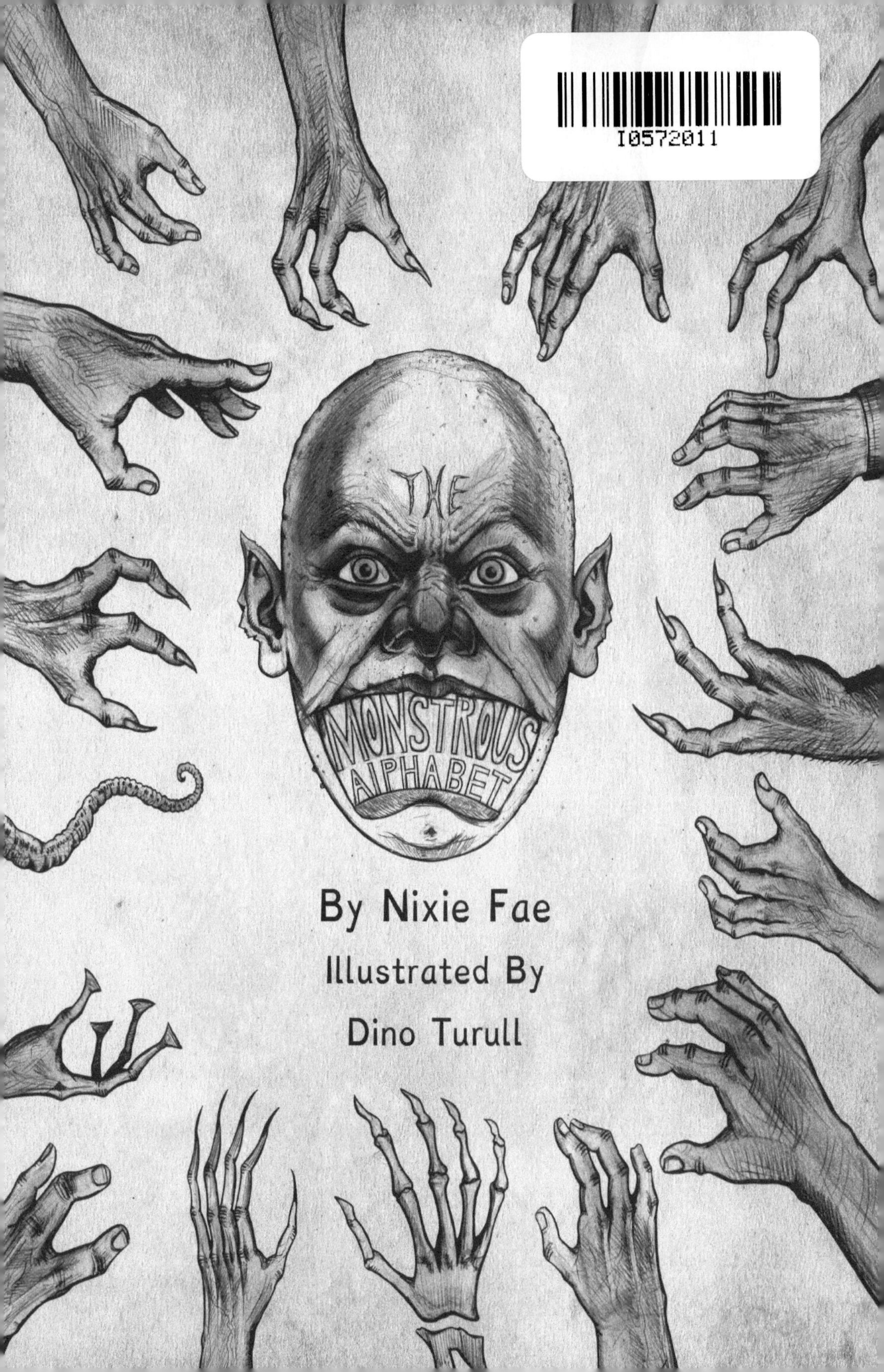
THE
MONSTROUS
ALPHABET
By Nixie Fae
Illustrated By
Dino Turull
I0572011

For the misunderstood weirdos who
also love books.
N.F.

To my father for his guidance through
the years.
D.T.

MacLaren-Cochrane Publishing, Inc.

Text©2017 Nixie Fae (Kenzie Derby)
Cover and Interior Art©2017 Dino Turull

The Monstrous Alphabet Dyslexic Edition

Library of Congress Control Number: 2017951948

Revised Edition

ISBN
Hardcover: 978-1-64372-275-7
Softcover: 978-1-64372-276-4

For orders, visit
www.mcp-store.com
www.maclaren-cochranepublishing.com
www.facebook.com/maclaren-cochranepublishing

You've probably read alphabets
Of the more normal type
Where **A** is for apple
And **B** is for bike
But this alphabet here
Won't be like that one bit
This alphabet is monstrous
Let's see where they fit

A Aswang – Filipino folklore

A is for Aswang
They're witches who eat
People's dead bodies
Including the feet

\ä swän\

B is for Banshee
A spirit who screams
When death is upon you
She may come in your dreams

\ban·shee\

C

Cambion – European mythology

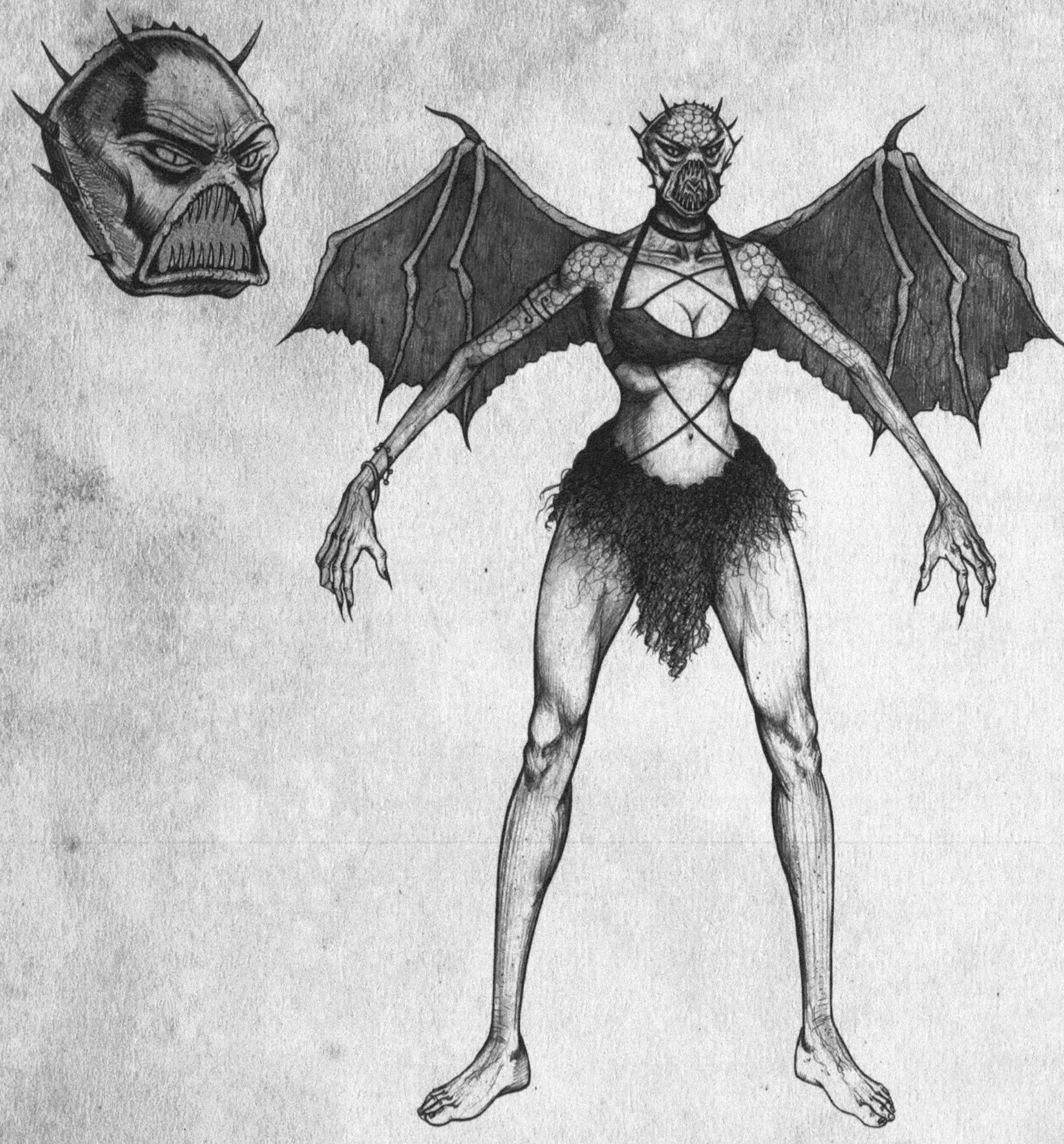

/ kæmbi n/

C is for Cambion
They're people like you
But half of their family
Has demon blood true.

D
Doppelganger - German

D is for Doppelganger
A shape shifter who,
Does all sorts of evil
While looking like you

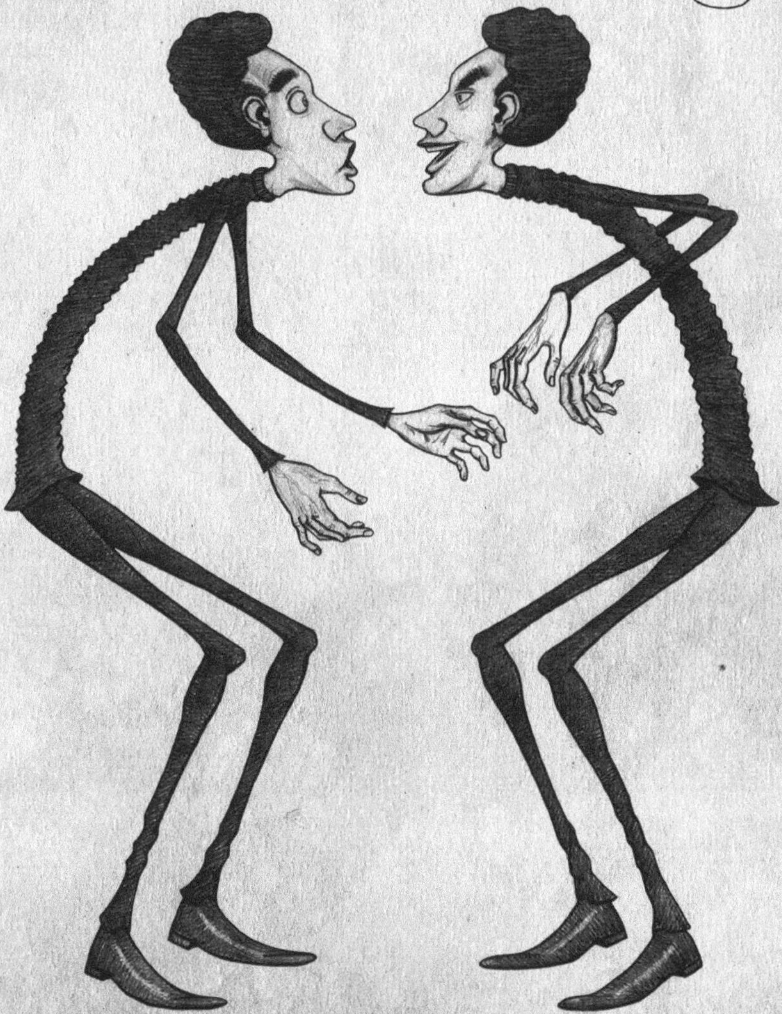

\ dop·pel·gäng·er \

E

Elemental –
Alchemy and
European folklore

E is for Elemental
A being who's constructed
From earth, water, or fire
And not easily disrupted

\ el·e·men·tal \

F

Funayurei –
Japanese Folklore

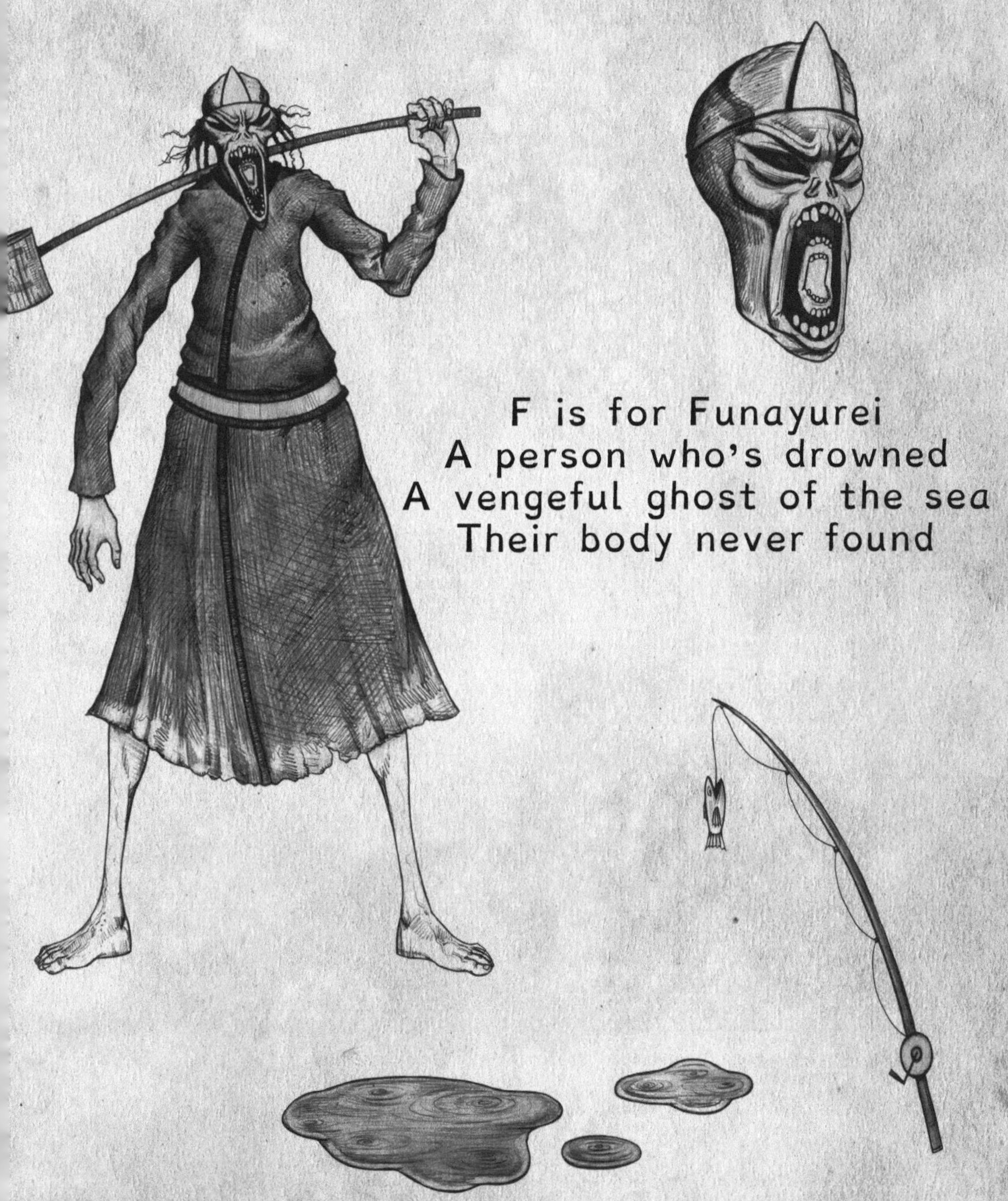

F is for Funayurei
A person who's drowned
A vengeful ghost of the sea
Their body never found

\Fun-a-yūr-ei\

G

Garuda – Hinduism

G is for Garuda
Half human half bird
They carry the gods
In case you hadn't heard

\ garud \

H

Hidebehind – American Folklore

H is for Hidebehind
a tall and slender beast
That hides behind trees
And waits for a feast

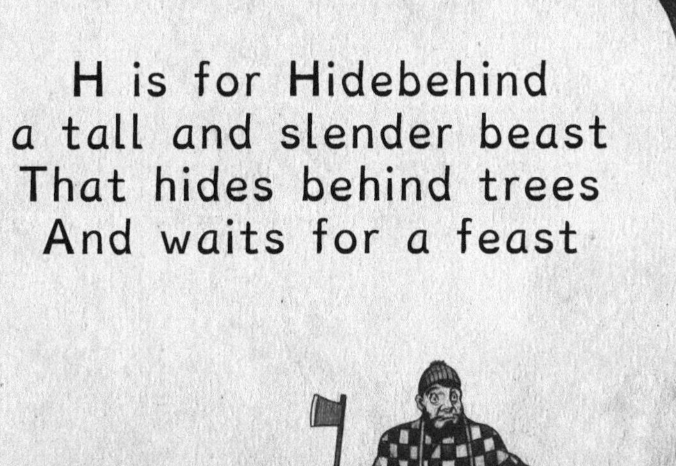

\ hīd be·hind\

Ifrit –
Middle Eastern Folklore

I is for Ifrit
A genie made of flame
Compared to other Jinn
They are much less tame

\ i,frēt \

J

Jerff –
Nordic Folklore

J is for Jerff
A mix of fox, dog, and cat
They eat and they eat
But they never get fat

\yerf\

K

Kelpie –
Scottish Folklore

\ kel-pē\

K is for Kelpie
A black horse that's swift
But don't climb on it's back
Or you'll be adrift

L
La llorona –
Hispanic American
Folklore

L is for La llorona
A spirit who weeps
To find her
drowned children
Their spirits to keep

\La Ya-rona\

M

Mogwai – Chinese Mythology

M is for Mogwai
A demon of mischief and charm
They take their vengeance on those
Who have caused them harm

\M-og-why\

N

Nixie –
Mixed European
Mythology

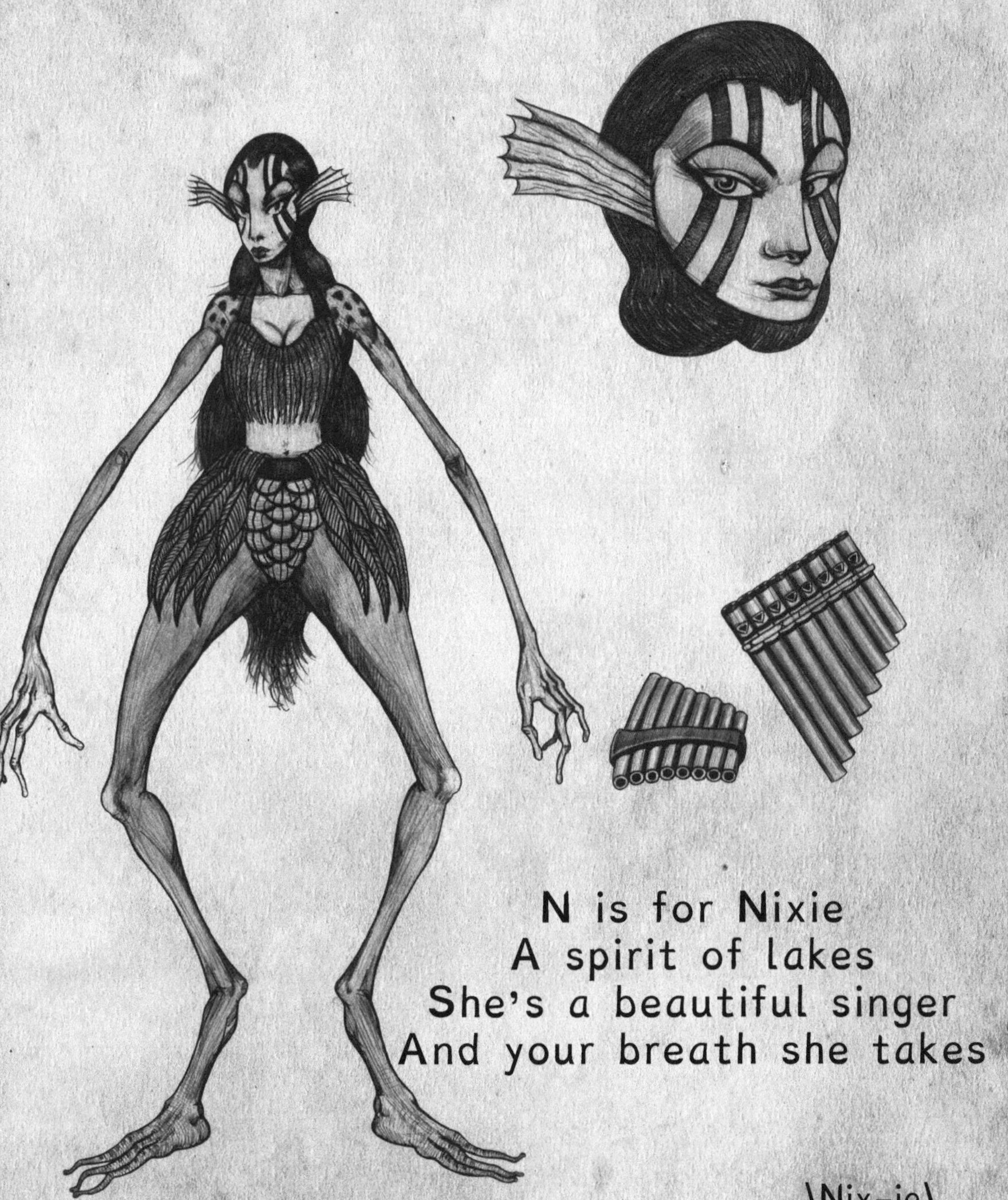

N is for Nixie
A spirit of lakes
She's a beautiful singer
And your breath she takes

\Nix-ie\

O

Odmience – Polish Mythology

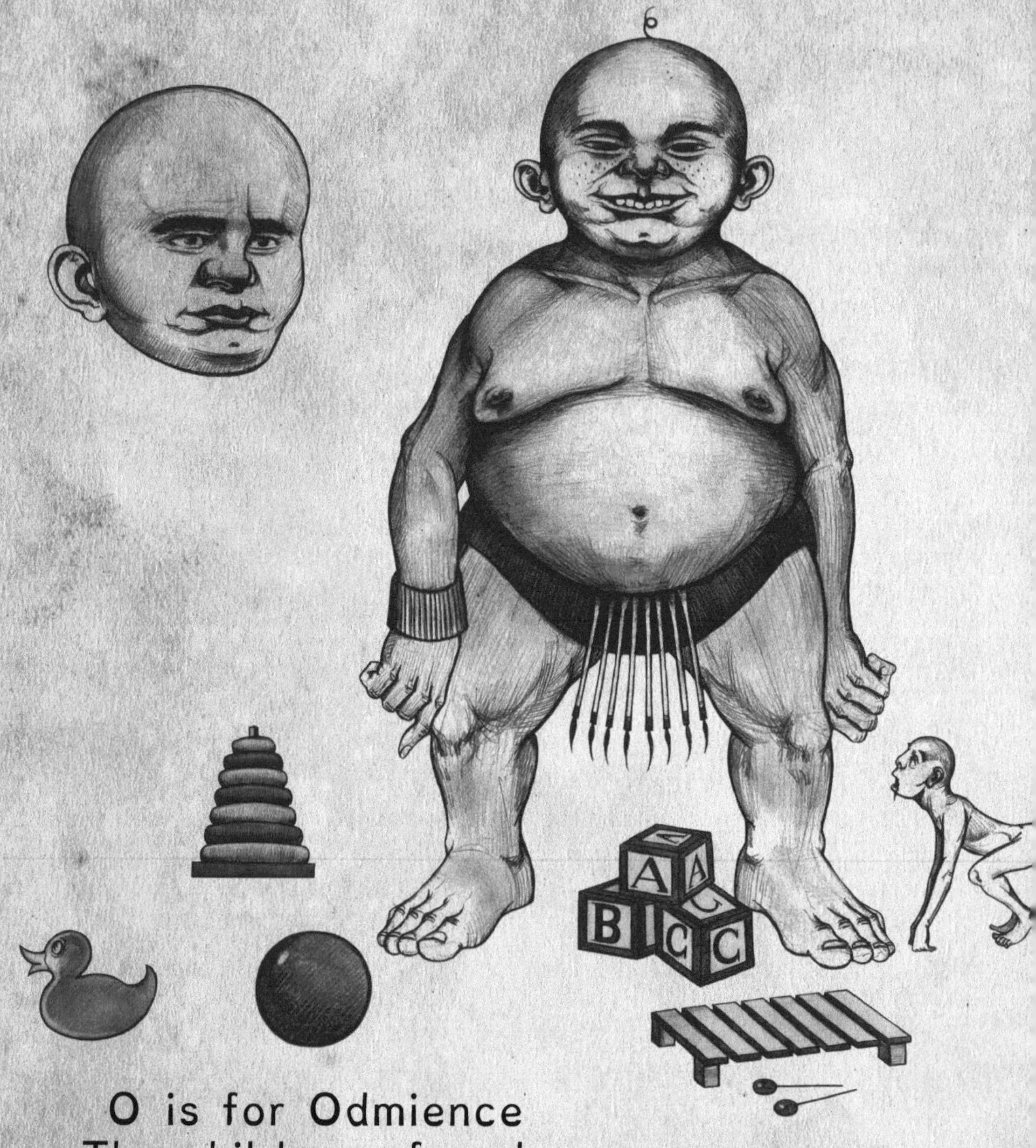

O is for Odmience
The children of gods
Put in the place of babies
What are the odds

\Od-mi-ence\

P Panis – Hinduism

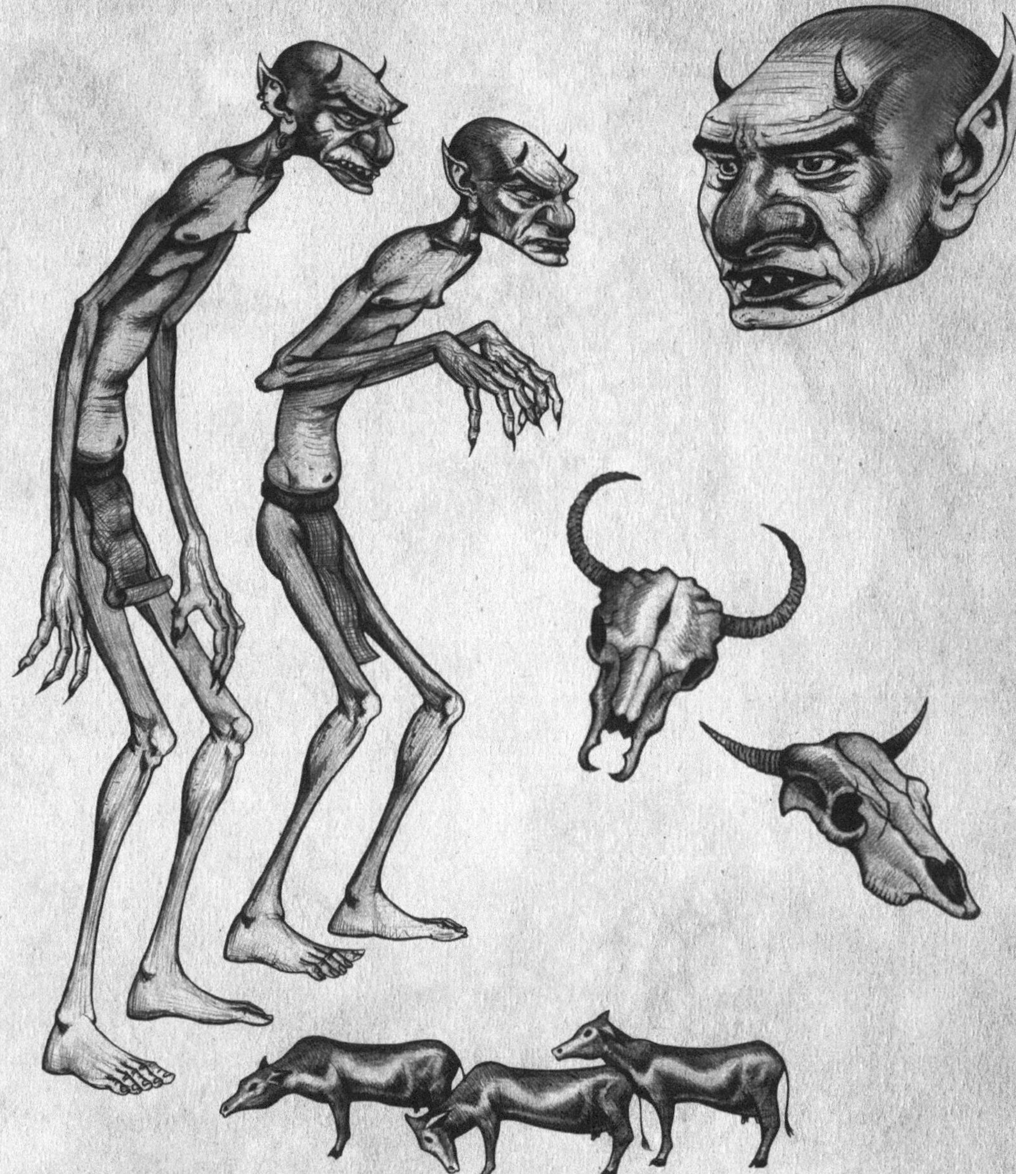

P is for Panis
Demonic thieves of sacred cattle
Armed with godly strength
They won't give them up without
a battle   \Pan-is\

Q
Qalupalik –
Inuit Mythology

Q is for Qalupalik
A green skinned woman from the sea
If you hear her humming
Childless you will be

\Ka-lu-pulic\

Raven Mocker – Native American Mythology

R is for Raven Mocker
On the old and the sick they feed
A fiery shape shifter
Your heart is all they need

\Raven Moncker\

S Santelmo – Filipino Mythology

S is for Santelmo
It's A blue ball of lightning
Or a pillar of dancing fire
The sight is frightening

\Sant-elmo\

T

Tsukumogami – Japanese Folklore

T is for Tsukumogami
An object with its own consciousness and life,
That it gained after a century
It strives for vengeance and strife

\schoo-mo-gami\

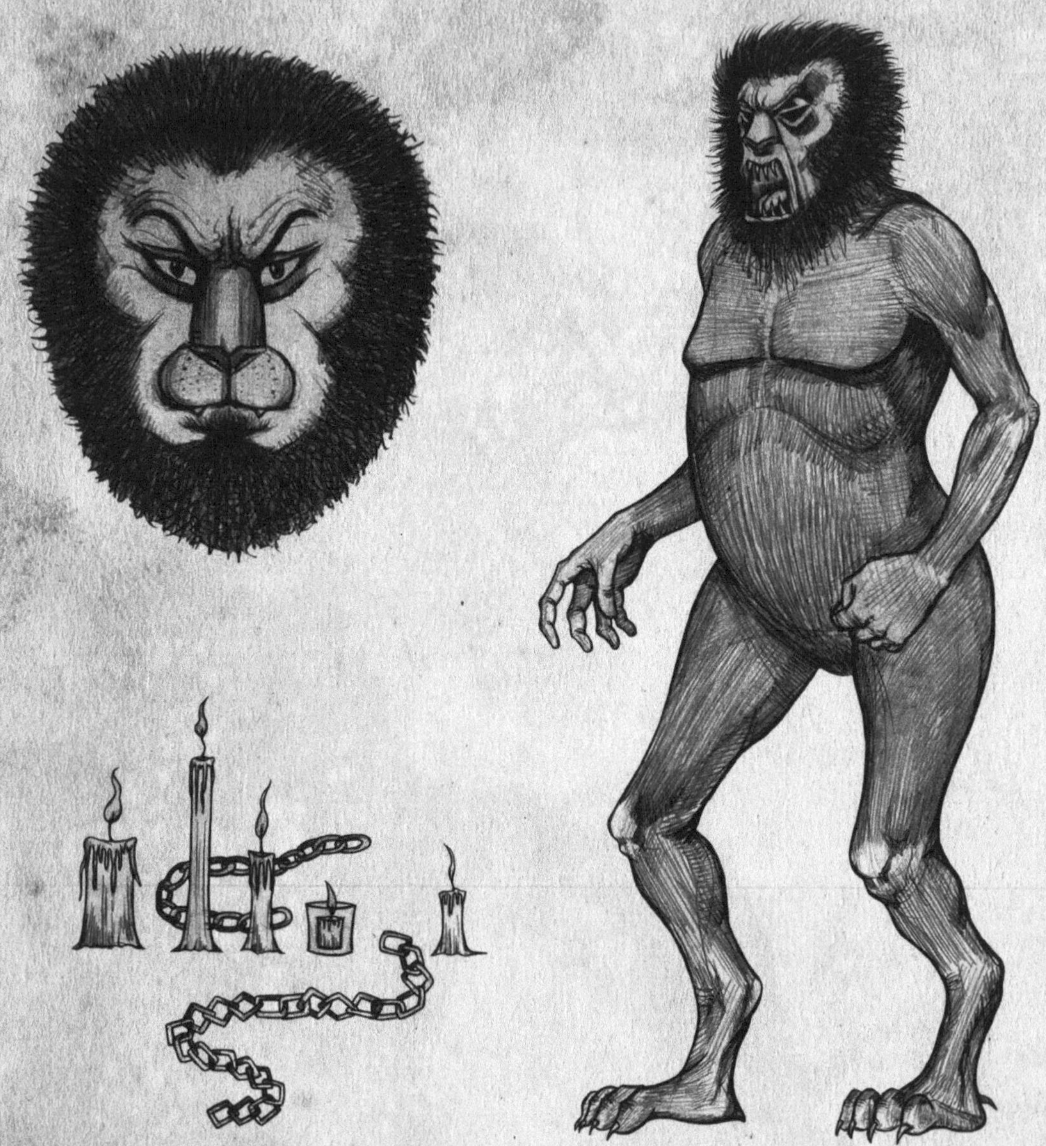

U

Utukku – Sumerian Mythology

U is for Utukku
It's a spirit of a man
Who's raised from the underworld
By a priests mighty hand

\u-ta-koo\

V

Valkyrie – Norse Mythology

V is for Valkyrie
A woman of war
If you see her in battle
You're on deaths door

\Val-kery\

W

Wendigo – Native American Folklore

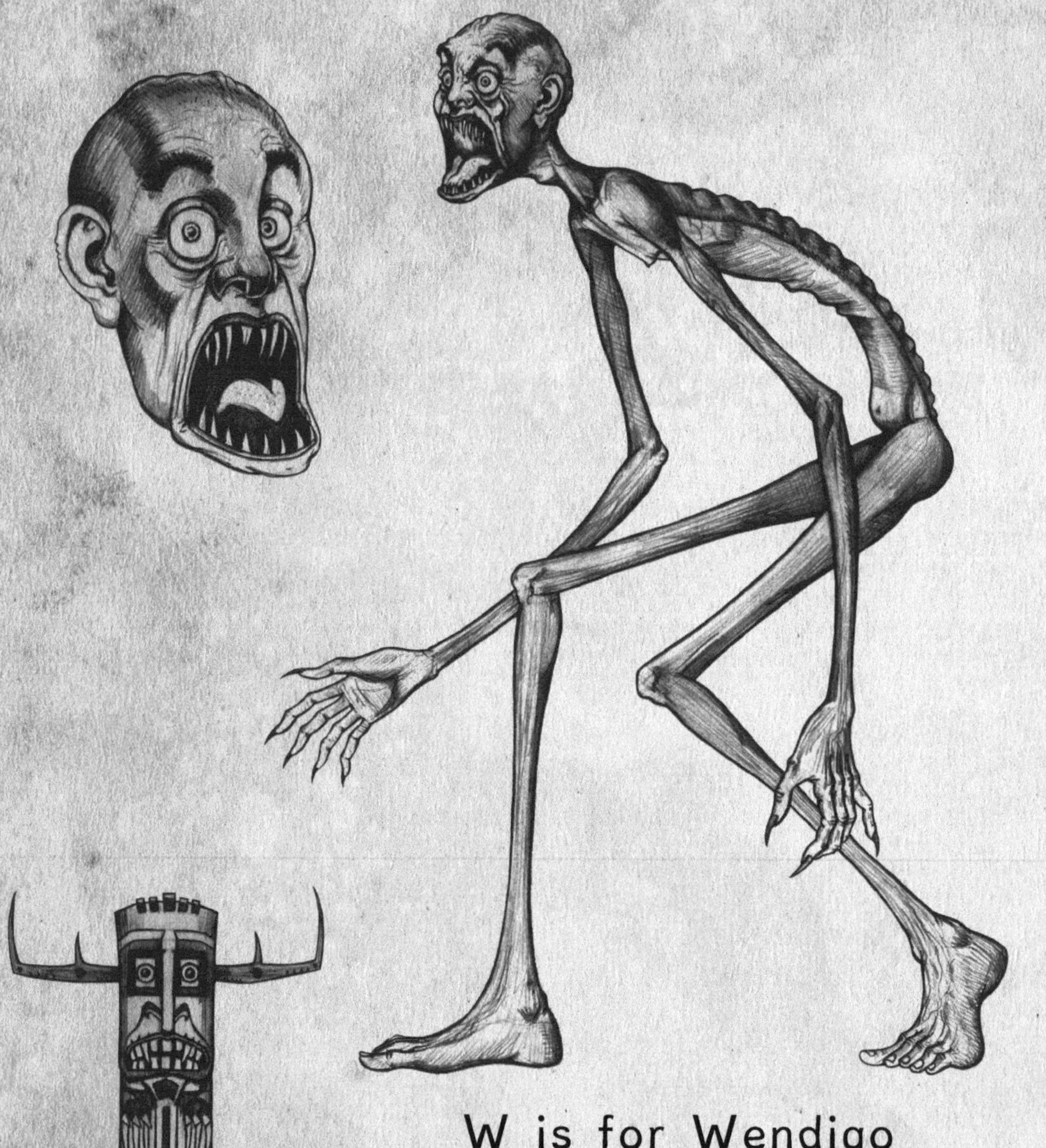

W is for Wendigo
They're mortal turned beast
They feed on flesh
And live in the east

\Win-da-go\

X

Xiuhcoatl – Aztec Mythology

X is for Xiuhcoatl
A serpent god of drought
There will be no water
When it is about

\Shem-ko-ach\

Y

Yaramayhawho – Australian Aboriginal Mythology

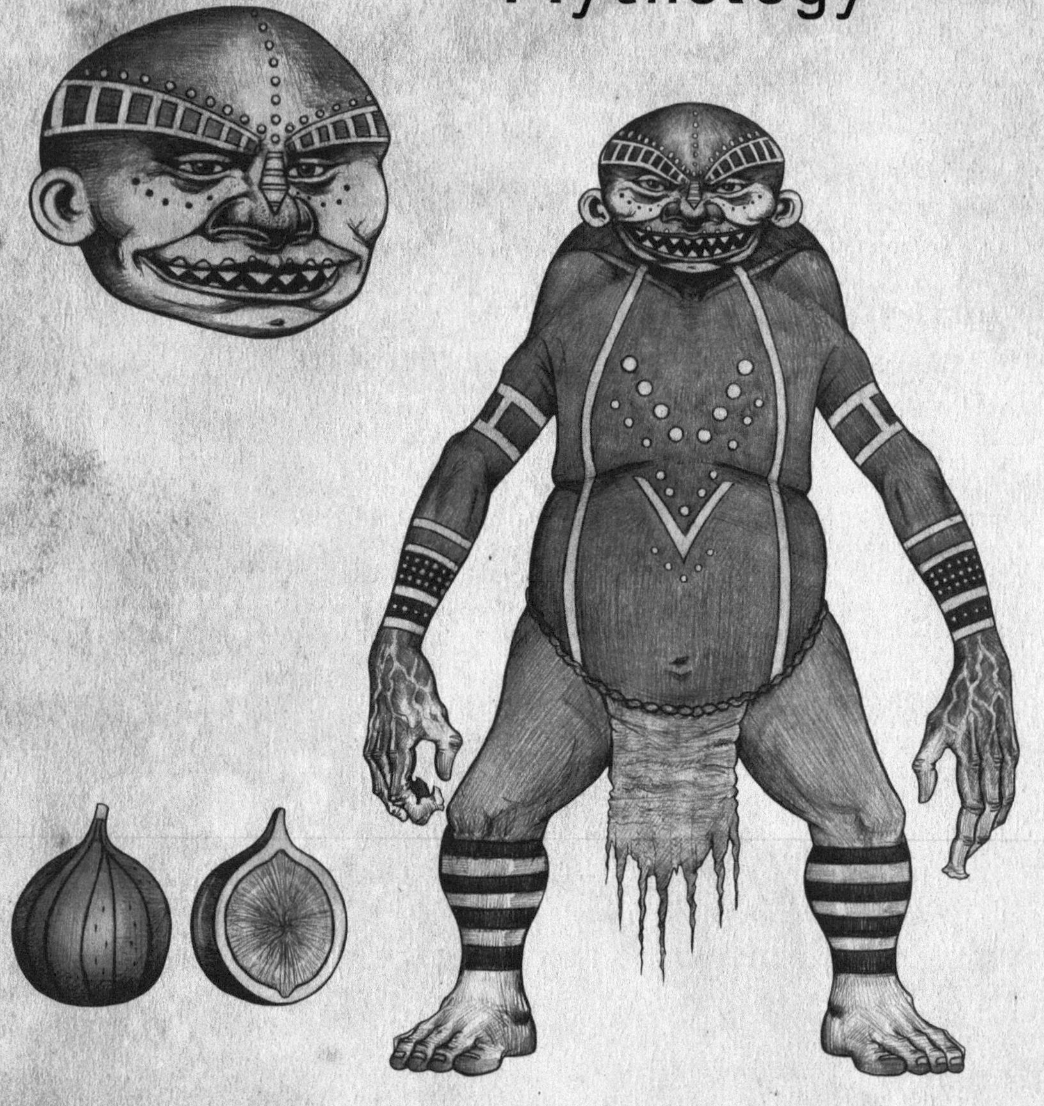

Y is for Yara-ma-yha-who
A little red man with suckers on his fingers
He drinks the blood of humans
And in fig trees he lingers

\ Yara-ma-yha-who\

Z

Zilant – Russian Mythology

Z is for Zilant
A winged serpent with bird talons
Banished to the bottom of a lake
It sleeps under the gallons

\Zi-lant\

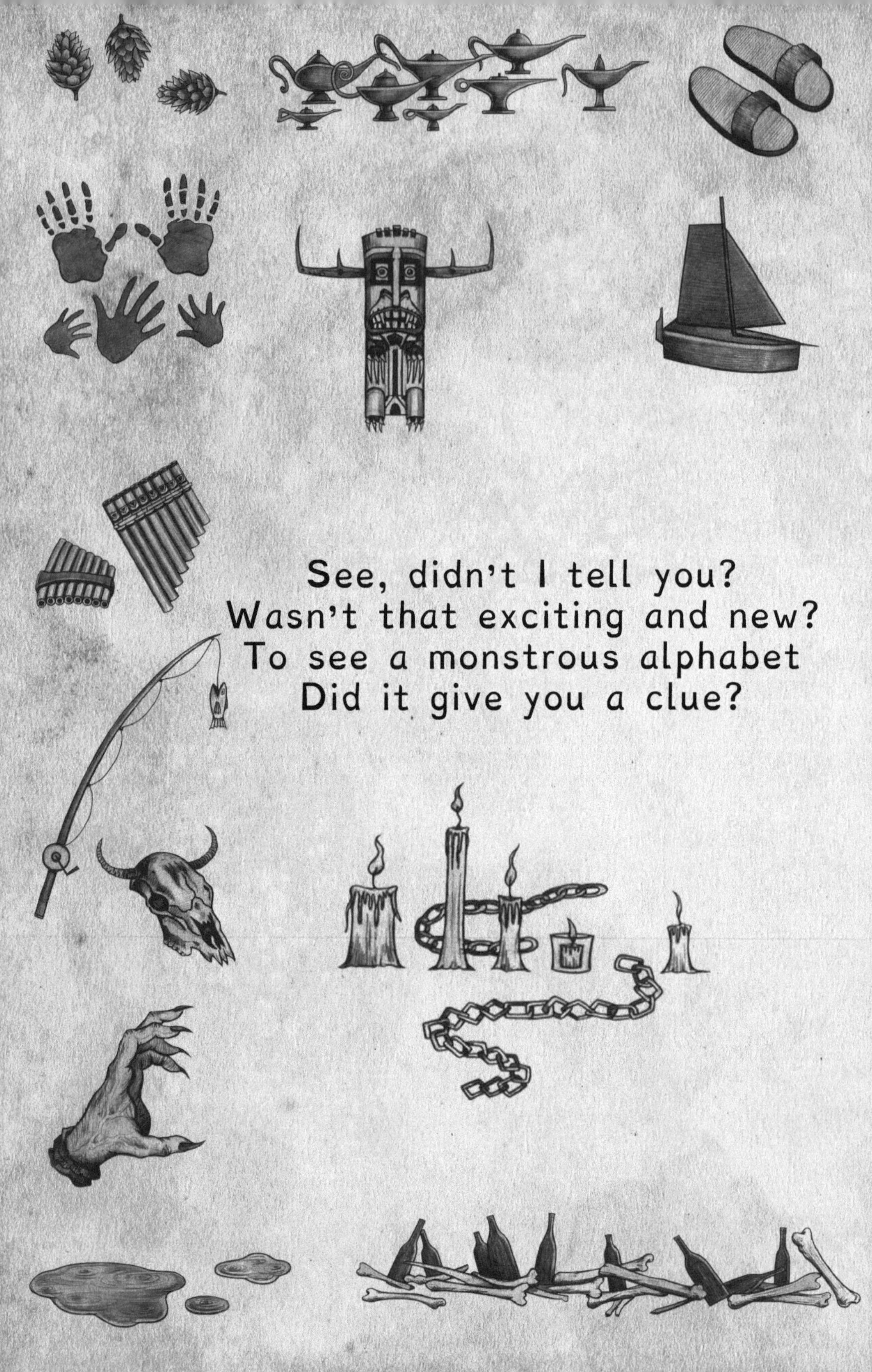

See, didn't I tell you?
Wasn't that exciting and new?
To see a monstrous alphabet
Did it give you a clue?

Not all alphabets are similar
And some, you might say are strange.
I've put all the monsters in place
Even if they had mange.

Glossary

A Aswang   \ä swäŋ\ Filipino folklore - A shapeshifting creature that possesses the attributes of a vampire and a witch. In different myths they feed on different things, some feed on dead bodies, others feed on unborn babies.

B Banshee \ban·shee\ Gaelic Folklore - A disheveled, sometimes haggish, woman who appears to people when they are doomed to die. She signifies this by letting out a 'wail', or a celtic funeral song.

C Cambion / kæmbi n/ European mythology - The child of a human and an incubus or succubus.

D Doppelganger \ dop·pel·gäng·er\ German - A person who may just extremely resemble someone else, or, a being that takes the form of one to slander their name.

E Elemental \ el·e·men·tal\ Alchemy and European folklore - A being constructed of any one element, brought to life via magic.

F Funayurei \Funayūrei\ Japanese Folklore - The ghost of someone who has been lost at sea.

G Garuda \ garud \ Hinduism - A large humanoid bird that the god Vishnu is depicted riding.

H Hidebehind   \ hīd be·hind\ American Folklore - A tall slender creature that uses its physique to hide behind trees and hunt down lumberjacks to eat.

I Ifrit \ i‚frēt \ Middle Eastern Folklore - Sometimes depicted as a large winged beast, and other times depicted as a type of djinn or genie, this creature is associated largely with fire and has a mischievous nature.

J Jerf f \yerf\ Nordic Folklore - More commonly referred to as a
'Gulon' this woodland carrion beast eats the bodies of dead animals. When
the creature becomes engorged with food it will shuffle itself
between two trees to force the food out.

K Kelpie \ kel-pē\ Scottish Folklore - Kelpies are most commonly
depicted as a black or dark colored horse, however they are water
 spirits who mean to drown you to feed on your body. They lure you onto
their backs and then run you into their body for water.

L La Llorona \La Ya-rona\ Hispanic American Folklore - The spirit
of a woman who drowned her two children to spite her unfaithful
 husband. After realizing what she had done she ended her own life, now
she searches for her lost children endlessly in the afterlife,
weeping for them eternally.

M Mogwai \M-og-why\ Chinese Mythology - Specific demonic
spirits that intend to inflict harm upon humans, specifically those who have
wronged them. They are thought to breed during the rain.

N Nixie \Nixie\ Mixed European mythology - A water spirit that takes
the form of a woman, sometimes frog or fish like in appearance. She presides
over a small body of freshwater, like a pond or stream. Nixies are mostly
docile but have been known for their curiosity and cunning.

O Odmience \Od-mi-ence\ Polish Mythology - A god or faery child put
in the place of a human one, commonly known as a 'changeling'.

P Panis \Pan-is\ Hinduism - A group of demons who watch over
stolen sacred cattle.

Q Qalupalik \Ka-lu-pulic\ Inuit Mythology - A long haired and green
skinned woman like creature that lives in the ocean, she steals bad children
from their parents. They are said to make a distinct
humming noise.

R Raven Mocker \Raven Moncker\ Native American Mythology –
A shapeshifting spirit who steals the hearts of the sick and elderly.

S Santelmo \Sant-elmo\ Filipino mythology – A floating ball of fire or
light, usually blue in color. Most commonly seen while sailing.

T Tsukumogami \schoo-mo-gami\ Japanese Folklore – An object that has
existed for one hundred years, thus gaining sentience. Commonly the objects
will try to take revenge on their owners.

U Utukku \u-ta-koo\ Sumerian Mythology – A spirit who had escaped from
the underworld either by the hand of a priest or on their own.

V Valkyrie \Val-kery\ Norse Mythology – A female spirit that takes the
spirits of warriors from battle. She escorts them to the afterlife of
warriors, Valhalla.

W Wendigo \Win-da-go\ Native American Folklore – A human that
undergoes physical changes after turning to cannibalism. The choice to eat
another human twists their body to mirror the monstrous act they have com-
mitted.

X Xiuhcoatl \Shem-ko-ach\ Aztec Mythology – The physical
embodiment of the aztec god of fire, a gigantic flying serpent. He would de-
scend from the sky and cause massive drought.

Y Yaramayhawho \ Yara-ma-yha-who\ Australian Aboriginal Mythology – A
small legendary creature that lives in fig trees. It's skin is bright red and it
drains humans of their blood via the suckers on its fingers and feet.

Z Zilant \Zi-lant\ Russian Mythology – A large serpent who sleeps at the
bottom of a lake. It has very large wings and a set of birdlike talons.

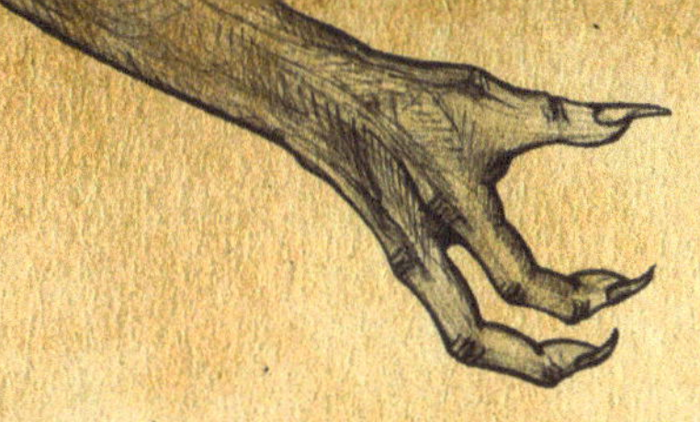

Nixie is a young writer that loves the world beyond our own. She is amazing in her descriptions and style. She loves teaching people about stuff that they would not usually have available to them. Kenzie has been writing stories, and poems from a very young age. She fell in love with the written word early and reads anything she can get her hands on.

It is not necessary to approach Dino Turull's images with knowledge of their sources. These figures and oddities create their own otherworldly atmosphere suitable to their own needs. Consisting of vibrant hues, illustrious backgrounds, and fantastic characters, these narrative artworks revel in their own cleverness. Technically and stylistically, they are brilliant. Playing with composition, he usually includes one to three focal points, depending on the story he is telling.

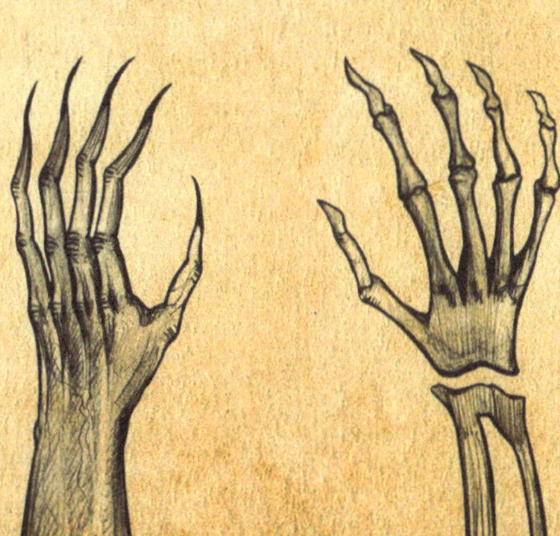

What is Dyslexie Font?

Each letter is given its own identity making it easier for people with dyslexia
to be more successful at reading.

The Dyslexie font:
1 Makes letters easier to distinguish
2 Offers more ease, regularity and joy in reading
3 Enables you to read with less effort
4 Gives your self-esteem a boost
5 Can be used anywhere, anytime and on (almost) every device
6 Does not require additional software or programs
7 Offers the simplest and most effective reading support

The Dyslexie font is specially designed for people with dyslexia, in order
to make reading easier - and more fun. During the design process, all
basic typography rules and standards were ignored. Readability and
specific characteristics of dyslexia are used as guidelines for the design.

Graphic designer Christian Boer created a dyslexic-friendly font to make reading easier for people
with dyslexia, like himself.

"Traditional fonts are designed solely from an aesthetic point of view," Boer writes on his website,
*"which means they often have characteristics that make characters difficult to recognize for people
with dyslexia. Oftentimes, the letters of a word are confused, turned around or jumbled up because
they look too similar."*

Designed to make reading clearer and more enjoyable for people with dyslexia, Dyslexie uses heavy
base lines, alternating stick and tail lengths, larger openings, and semicursive slants to ensure that
each character has a unique and more easily recognizable form.

Our books are not just for children to enjoy, they are also for adults
who have dyslexia who want the experience of reading
to the children in their lives.

Learn more and get the font for your digital devices at
www.dyslexiefont.com

Get books in Dyslexie Font at: www.mcp-store.com

Short paragraphs, chapters, and
exciting themes for the perfect
bridge to chapter books.

9 781643 722764